A Whale of a Tale

★ Also by ★
Debbie Dadey

MERMAID TALES, BOOK 1:
TROUBLE AT TRIDENT ACADEMY

MERMAID TALES, BOOK 2:
BATTLE OF THE BEST FRIENDS

Mermaid Tales

★ Debbie Dadey ★

Illustrated by
Tatevik Avakyan

BOOK
3

A Whale of a Tale

ALADDIN

NEW YORK   LONDON   TORONTO   SYDNEY   NEW DELHI

ALADDIN

An imprint of Simon & Schuster Children's Publishing Division
1230 Avenue of the Americas, New York, NY 10020
First Aladdin paperback edition August 2012
Text copyright © 2012 by Debbie Dadey
Illustrations copyright © 2012 by Tatevik Avakyan
All rights reserved, including the right of reproduction in whole or in part in any form.
ALADDIN is a trademark of Simon & Schuster, Inc.,
and related logo is a registered trademark of Simon & Schuster, Inc.
Also available in an Aladdin hardcover edition.
For information about special discounts for bulk purchases,
please contact Simon & Schuster Special Sales at 1-866-506-1949
or business@simonandschuster.com.
The Simon & Schuster Speakers Bureau can bring authors to
your live event. For more information or to book an event contact the
Simon & Schuster Speakers Bureau at 1-866-248-3049 or visit
our website at www.simonspeakers.com.
Designed by Karin Paprocki
The text of this book was set in Belucian Book.
Manufactured in the United States of America 0814 OFF
4 6 8 10 9 7 5
Library of Congress Control Number 2012936946
ISBN 978-1-4424-5318-0 (hc)
ISBN 978-1-4424-2984-0 (pbk)
ISBN 978-1-4424-2985-7 (eBook)

To my nephew Damon Gibson,
who swam with humpback whales
and was kind enough
to tell me about it

✦ ✦ ✦ ✦

Acknowledgment

Thank you to my husband, Eric Dadey, for
putting up with me for twenty-nine years
of marriage.

Cast of Characters

Shelly

Echo

Kiki

Pearl

Rocky

Contents

1	OCEAN TRIP	1
2	DR. MOUSTEAU	6
3	FUNNY NOISES	13
4	KILLER WHALE	22
5	LUCKY CHARM	33
6	TO THE TOP	42
7	NO MORE SECRETS	49
8	WHALE RIDE	56
9	DEEP-SEA DANGER	61
10	A BIG DECISION	64
11	FLYING	76
12	TROUBLE TIME?	82
	CLASS REPORTS	91
	THE MERMAID TALES SONG	95
	AUTHOR'S NOTE	97
	GLOSSARY	99

A Whale of a Tale

Ocean Trip

ROCKY RIDGE WASN'T HAPPY. "Do we have to do another project?" he whined to his teacher. "Mrs. Karp, that's not fair!"

In the first few weeks of the new school year at Trident Academy, Mrs. Karp's third-grade class had already completed reports on famous merpeople and a project where they'd collected krill and shrimp. Every one of the twenty students hoped they wouldn't have to do another big assignment.

Mrs. Karp smiled. "This lesson is different. We're going on an ocean trip."

Rocky and the rest of the class cheered. "Yes! Awesome!"

Kiki Coral gasped. But her mergirl friends Echo Reef and Shelly Siren clapped their hands and swished their tails. For many in the class, this would be their first ocean trip. They would leave classwork behind to learn in a deep-sea environment. "It's about time we did something fun," a mergirl named Pearl Swamp snapped.

"Where are we going, Mrs. Karp?" Kiki asked.

"An article in the *Trident City Tide* reported that a pod of whales is expected to be directly above Trident City tomorrow

morning. We will visit them. In fact, Dr. Evan Mousteau will join us in a few minutes to tell us about whales and even teach us a bit of whale language."

Mrs. Karp continued, "I expect you to be courteous to Dr. Mousteau. After he leaves, we'll go over surface safety rules. Your parents can feel secure that the guards from the Shark Patrol will be on the alert all morning, not only for sharks, but also for any sign of humans."

Echo could barely speak. "Humans!" she whispered to Shelly and Kiki. "I've always wanted to see a real, live human. Maybe tomorrow will be my chance!" Everything about humans fascinated Echo.

"Are you sure it's safe? My parents

have never let me go above water," Echo said to Mrs. Karp.

Mrs. Karp patted Echo on the shoulder. "Don't worry, we will only go if it is safe."

Then Kiki shyly asked, "Which whale dialect will we be learning?"

Mrs. Karp raised her green eyebrows. "Excellent question. I wonder how many of you know that whales talk to one another?"

No one raised their hand except Shelly. Kiki smiled at her.

"Since the visiting pod is made up of humpbacks, we will focus on the humpback whale dialect," Mrs. Karp told the class.

Kiki nodded, still smiling, but in truth she was worried. Really worried.

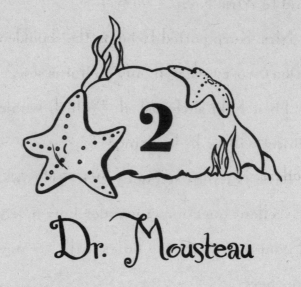

Dr. Mousteau

DR. MOUSTEAU REMINDED Kiki of the bottlenose dolphins that lived near her home in the far-off waters by Asia. He had the same shiny bald head and long pointed nose. Even his eyes were round and black. Kiki wondered if Dr. Mousteau had twenty-five pairs of teeth in each jaw. When he opened his mouth, she got her answer: He had one big tooth in the center of his top gum. That was it.

"The humpback whale is a wondrous creature," Dr. Mousteau told the third graders. "The pattern of white markings on the flukes and flippers is different on each and every whale. So no two whales are alike."

Dr. Mousteau continued, "Adult humpbacks are quite large and weigh ten times more than a great white shark."

"Those whales need to go on a diet," Rocky blurted out.

Mrs. Karp frowned, but Dr. Mousteau didn't seem to mind Rocky's interruption.

He went on, "As you might know, man is the only predator of whales. Thankfully, humans' captures of whales in recent years have decreased. Still, the humpback population is about one-fifth of what it was hundreds of years ago."

Dr. Mousteau reached into a bag and took out a thick piece of skin. "I'd like each of you to touch the specimen I'm passing around. This was taken from a whale that died naturally. I brought it for you to study."

Dr. Mousteau gave the skin to Rocky, who felt and even sniffed it. Rocky tried to give it to Pearl, but she shook her head. "I don't want to touch any disgusting dead whale. It has awful bumps and nasty barnacles on it."

"That's quite normal," Dr. Mousteau said, taking the specimen and handing it to Shelly. "Every humpback has a long head with knobs such as these. If you didn't clean yourselves thoroughly, you'd have barnacles too."

"I had a barnacle one time," Rocky said, "but my dad made me wash it off."

Shelly felt the whale skin and tried to give it to Kiki, but Kiki's eyes were glued to Dr. Mousteau. "Here, Kiki," Shelly said, but Kiki wouldn't look.

Shelly shrugged and passed the skin to Echo, who took it with two fingers and quickly gave it to a mergirl named Morgan. Morgan only looked at it for a second before handing it to a merboy named Adam.

Kiki shuddered. She'd almost had to touch the whale skin. She hoped that wouldn't happen again. She tried to concentrate on Dr. Mousteau's lessons on water pressure and whale speech, even though she spoke humpback perfectly. Pearl and Echo giggled as they tried to imitate the strange sounds. Rocky sounded more like a sick seal than a whale. Shelly was surprisingly good.

After the language lesson, Dr. Mousteau said, "If you are very lucky tomorrow, three things might happen."

"What are they?" Pearl asked. "I want to be lucky."

Dr. Mousteau smiled, showing the one tooth in the middle of his mouth. "First, you may see a whale jumping out of the water."

"That's known as breaching," added Mrs. Karp.

"Cool," Rocky said.

"Number two," Dr. Mousteau said, "you may hear the males sing."

"Do the females sing?" Shelly asked.

"No," Dr. Mousteau said.

"That's not fair. Why not?" Shelly asked.

Mrs. Karp explained, "The males sing to attract females."

Dr. Mousteau nodded in agreement before continuing. "And three, if you are very lucky, you may see a baby whale."

Echo looked at Kiki. "Wouldn't that be great? Babies are so cute."

Kiki swallowed hard. "Sure," she said. But Kiki didn't think baby whales would be cute at all. In fact, whales of any size absolutely terrified her.

Funny Noises

"THIS IS AWESOME," ECHO TOLD Kiki and Shelly in the Trident Academy lunchroom that afternoon.

Kiki looked up from her lunch of polkadot batfish sushi in surprise. "What do you mean? This is the worst sushi they've served all year."

"I'm not talking about the food, Kiki," Echo said. "I mean the ocean trip. Maybe I'll finally get to see people! I'd like to see a baby whale, and I've never been to the surface before. It's exciting."

Shelly swallowed her octopus legs and licked her fingers. "I can't wait. I've always wanted to swim with whales."

"Swim with them? I could never do that!" Echo squealed. "My dad made me do a report on them last year in second grade. Do you know how big they are?"

Kiki nodded. "Whales are the largest creatures that have ever lived. That's why Mrs. Karp wants us to study them." Kiki didn't tell the girls that she was scared, but she was glad to hear that Echo was a little bit afraid too.

"They do this thing called bubble netting, where they trap their food!" Echo told her friends. Kiki stopped eating and stared at her.

Shelly shook her head. "Don't worry. Whales only eat fish and krill."

Echo flipped her pink mermaid tail. "Excuse me, but don't we look like big fish?"

Kiki looked down at her purple tail and gulped. Humpback whales were huge. All they had to do to swallow a mermaid was open their gigantic mouths wide. She was the smallest merkid in their class. What if a whale mistook her for a snack? Kiki closed her eyes for a moment and shuddered.

"I thought you wanted to see humans," Shelly said to Echo.

Echo smiled and pushed her dark, curly hair off her forehead. "You know it."

"Well, this could be your only chance," Shelly said. "My grandfather says humans love to watch whales."

Echo giggled. "Really? Then I can't miss the trip. I'd do almost anything to see a real, live human." She clasped her hands together, and Kiki could tell that Echo had forgotten her fear of whales in her excitement about seeing a human. Kiki felt totally alone with her secret. What was she going to do tomorrow? She just wasn't ready to share her fears.

"Now that that's settled, let's make Mr. Fangtooth smile today," Shelly told her friends. Ever since school had started a few weeks ago, the girls had tried to make the grumpy lunchroom worker cheer up. On the first day of school, they'd made funny faces at him. That had made him laugh, but it had also gotten them sent to the headmaster's office. Another time, Kiki and Shelly had walked on their hands in front of Mr. Fangtooth, but that had made him frown even more.

"I know," Kiki suggested, glad to think of something besides whales. "We could make weird sounds."

"What do you mean?" Shelly asked.

"At home, when it was time to sleep, my seventeen brothers would make silly noises one by one, and by the time they got to number seventeen, we were laughing so hard my dad would have to yell at everyone to go to sleep. But then he'd make the silliest sound of all, and we'd start laughing all over again." Remembering those good times made Kiki miss her family. The Trident Academy dorm room was a long way from her home.

Shelly giggled. "Let's try it." Shelly, Echo, and Kiki glided over to return their lunch trays. Mr. Fangtooth stood behind the rock counter, wearing his usual frown.

"BBBBBLLLLLLLLSSSS," Kiki said as

she put down her tray. Her lips jiggled like a motorboat. Mr. Fangtooth didn't laugh, but everyone else in the lunchroom did.

"What was that?" shouted Rocky from a nearby table. "Did you hear what Kiki did?"

A table full of mergirls, headed by Pearl, pointed at Kiki and laughed. Kiki rushed back to her seat and covered her face with her long hair. "I'm so embarrassed," she said.

"Don't worry," Shelly told Kiki. "Rocky will find someone else to tease before long." Rocky was always making mischief.

"He'll be so excited about seeing the whales tomorrow, he won't think about you," Echo pointed out.

Kiki faked a smile for her friends. Trying to cheer up Mr. Fangtooth had made her forget about her fear of whales for a minute. Now she remembered again, and her stomach did a flip-flop.

She knew she was being silly. After all, whales were known for being gentle. But they were so *big*! And she was so small. She couldn't help how she felt any more than she could help how little she was.

Kiki put her head down. Her stomach was hurting, and it wasn't from the sushi. She had to think of a way to get out of the ocean trip tomorrow, and she had to think fast.

Killer Whale

AFTER SCHOOL, KIKI AND SHELLY met under Trident Academy's massive entrance dome. A glowing jellyfish chandelier lit up the colorful carvings on the ceiling. "Do you want to come to my dorm room while Echo's at Tail Flippers practice?" Kiki asked Shelly. Echo and Shelly had been friends since they'd been small fry, but Kiki had met the girls only a few weeks before, when school had started.

Shelly smiled. "Sure! I'd love to see your room." Shelly and Echo lived just a short swim away from Trident Academy, but many mergirls and merboys lived far from school and had to stay in the dormitory. Since Kiki's home was thousands of miles away near Asia, she lived in the dorm.

"It's not that exciting," Kiki admitted as they swam toward the girls' dorm. It was a short distance from the classrooms, down a long hallway, past a seaweed curtain marked MERGIRLS ONLY. The boys' rooms were on the opposite side of the school.

"I bet it's better than my apartment," Shelly said.

"At the People Museum?" Kiki asked.

"Yes," Shelly said. "I live with my grandfather. Our place is on the second floor." Shelly had lived with her grandfather since her parents died. The People Museum was filled with human objects of all sorts that had been found throughout the ocean. Merpeople came from all over the merkingdom to visit and study.

"Wow, that sounds neat," Kiki said as the mergirls floated down the hallway to the rooms. Some girls had decorated their seaweed doors with shell carvings of their families. One girl had even braided a pretty gold chain into her seaweed.

Shelly shook her head. "I think human stuff is boring. Echo loves it. But humans can't even swim."

"I've heard that some can," Kiki said.

"I hope so," Shelly said. "I can't imagine not being able to swim. Wouldn't it be horrible?"

Kiki stopped in front of a bright-blue shell curtain, pulled it back, and said, "Here's my room." One side of the room was filled with fluffy pink coral and tube sponges. Sparkling jewel anemones covered one wall. Merclothes littered the floor. "That's my roommate Wanda Slug's side," Kiki sighed as she looked at the mess.

"Is this yours?" Shelly asked, and pointed across the room to an enormous skeleton. "Is that a shark?"

"It's my bed!" Kiki explained. "It might look like a shark, but it's actually a killer whale. Come on, you can sit on it." The two girls crawled inside the ribs of the huge skeleton and sank into a nest of feathers.

"Wow, this is soft," Shelly said.

"My mermom saved gray heron feathers for five years to make this bed for me," Kiki said.

"You should come over to my apartment for dinner sometime," Shelly suggested. "My grandfather, Siren, would enjoy

meeting you. He loves learning about far-away waters."

"Your grandfather is the famous C. Siren, right?"

Shelly nodded. "Yes, it's kind of embarrassing."

"I think it would be cool to have a human expert in the family," Kiki said.

"I'm more interested in how you got this skeleton," Shelly said. "I bet Echo would never crawl inside this in a hundred years. Sharks and killer whales give her the creeps."

"Wanda hates it too. She says it gives her nightmares," Kiki told Shelly.

Shelly laughed. "I bet it was funny to see her face when she got a look at this." She gently patted one of the big rib bones.

"Are you scared of killer whales and sharks?" Kiki asked.

Shelly shrugged. "I'd be crazy not to be. They're pretty dangerous. But skeletons can't hurt you."

"That's true," Kiki said. "But what about whales? Are you scared of whales? They're enormous!" Kiki held her breath as she waited for Shelly's answer. Maybe she'd be able to tell Shelly how she really felt.

"Of course not. Why would I be?" Shelly said. "Whales are amazing. My grandfather taught me to speak the humpback dialect. I'm going to try to talk to one tomorrow."

"Really?" Kiki said. "I can speak humpback too!" Languages had always come easily to Kiki. Her father was an expert linguist who had taught her more than fifty undersea languages.

"Awesome. Tomorrow, let's talk to the humpbacks together," Shelly said as she got off the bed and floated to the front curtain. "Unless . . . unless you're afraid of whales. Are you?"

Kiki stared at Shelly. If Kiki told her the truth, Shelly might make fun of her and tell all the other third graders. How would Kiki ever go to class again?

"No way," Kiki answered. "I can't wait until tomorrow. I'll be there early!"

AFTER SHELLY LEFT, KIKI STAYED ON HER skeleton bed, safe and secure in the soft feathers. She had never felt smaller or more afraid. *What will I do about the class trip?* she thought. *Those whales are so gigantic! They could swallow someone my size in one gulp. I wish my parents were here to help me.*

Kiki put her hand under her pillow. She felt around for a few seconds, then took out a small coral-colored shell purse.

She opened it up. Inside was an orange starfish, tiny and delicate. Kiki held it up to her cheek. Her mother had given it to her before Kiki set off for Trident Academy, as a reminder of home and as a good-luck charm.

Kiki hoped its luck would help her tomorrow. She would need it more than ever.

5

Lucky Charm

THE NEXT MORNING, MRS. KARP'S third-grade class arrived at Trident Academy earlier than usual. Everyone was excited about seeing the whales, and there was a nervous buzz in the swirling waters.

"Quiet down, quiet down, and listen

closely," Mrs. Karp told her students as they gathered outside the school. "I am handing each of you an ID tag to clip to your tail. This is your identification for the Shark Patrol." She handed out gold coins that had been folded to snap onto the students' tail fins. The coins were marked with the Trident Academy symbol.

Mrs. Karp was counting the mergirls and merboys. When she got to Shelly and Echo, she stopped. "Has either of you seen Kiki?"

Shelly answered, "No, Mrs. Karp. She told me yesterday she'd be here first thing in the morning."

"We won't leave without her, will we?"

Echo asked. "Please, let's just wait a few more minutes."

"No way! No way!" yelled Pearl. She dashed over to Mrs. Karp and the girls, her long pearl necklace trailing behind her. "Why should we let Kiki ruin the trip for us?"

Rocky joined in. "Yeah, Mrs. Karp. That little squirt is probably too scared to show up!"

Mrs. Karp clapped her hands three times. "We will wait two more minutes for Kiki, and then I'm afraid we'll have to go," she announced.

The class lined up two by two, Shelly and Echo in the rear. Just when the friends thought they would have to leave, they heard a splash behind them.

It was Kiki! Out of breath and looking as pale as mother-of-pearl, the little mergirl swam over to her friends, her head down.

"Where have you been?" Shelly said. "You had us worried."

Echo called out to Mrs. Karp, "Kiki's here! Let's go!"

Rocky looked over his shoulder and blurted out, "It's about time, shrimp! Who do you think you are, anyway—Neptune?"

"Rocky, that will be enough out of you," Mrs. Karp said sharply, and handed Kiki an ID tag. "I expect everyone to be on their best behavior."

"Are you feeling okay?" Shelly whispered to Kiki.

Kiki didn't lie. "No, I feel terrible. My stomach really hurts. That's why I'm so late."

"Maybe you shouldn't go," Shelly suggested. "I could stay with you."

Kiki smiled at her friend. She knew how badly Shelly wanted to see the whales.

"No," Echo said. "You go, Shelly. I'll take Kiki back to her dorm room."

Now Kiki smiled at Echo. Kiki knew that Echo hoped to see humans at the surface, even if just for a minute. Kiki couldn't ask her friends to give up this adventure. "That's okay. I'm sure I'll be fine." Kiki nodded at her teacher but held her arms around her stomach.

Mrs. Karp said to the class, "Now that
Kiki's arrived, we can be on our way."

"All right!" Rocky shouted.

Mrs. Karp frowned and continued, "Listen carefully to these important instructions before we go. The sunlight is very strong, so keep your eyes closed at first. You may swim around to study the whales, but do not wander far. I will blow the conch horn when it's time to return below to school." Mrs. Karp patted the shell she had slung around her shoulder.

"I hope I can do this," Echo whispered. "I'm excited, but I'm also a little nervous."

Shelly patted Echo's arm. "Don't worry. We'll stay with you, right, Kiki?"

Kiki nodded. She thought Echo was brave to admit she was a tiny bit scared. Why couldn't she do the same?

"If there are humans around, I will blow two quick blasts on the shell and we will immediately submerge," Mrs. Karp added. No one needed to be told about the dangers of humans seeing merkids.

Echo's tail fluttered. "Let's hope there are humans and we can get a quick peek," she whispered to her friends.

Shelly nodded. "Grandpa told me humans like to watch humpbacks because they breach so often."

Shelly held out one hand to Echo, the other to Kiki. Kiki held on to Shelly, her shell purse swinging back and forth on her wrist. Kiki closed her eyes and wished to herself, *Please let me be brave.*

To the Top

REMEMBER, YOU MAY EXPERIENCE some discomfort on the way to the surface," Mrs. Karp told the class.

"Discomfort?" Kiki said, popping her eyes open and growing paler. "That doesn't sound good."

"It's all right," Shelly told her. "If your stomach feels worse, just tell us."

"Pay close attention to the whales," Mrs. Karp continued. "When we get back to school, you will write an essay on your experiences."

Rocky couldn't believe his ears. "An essay?" he groaned. "I knew this was too good to be true."

Kiki's throat got tighter and tighter. She felt as if she was going to pass out. She had seen whales from far away, and that had scared her. Now she was going to be close. Too close.

"When I count to three, you may swim to the surface," Mrs. Karp instructed. "One, two . . ."

"I think I'm going to throw up," Kiki whimpered to herself.

"Three!" Mrs. Karp said.

Several mergirls squealed. Some of the merboys cheered. But they all began rising in the water.

Merfolk live in the deep parts of the ocean, for protection from sharks and humans, and their eyes are used to the darkness. Even so, Kiki accidentally bumped an old merwoman, who shook her finger at the entire class. "You should be in school instead of knocking decent merfolk about."

"S-sorry," Kiki stammered.

"I've seen that lady near the Manta Ray Station," Shelly whispered.

Pearl and Wanda swam by. "What a grouch," Pearl said.

Wanda chimed in, "She should meet Mr. Fangtooth." Both mergirls laughed as they passed Kiki and her friends.

As the class got closer to the top, the water became clearer and quite bright.

"I'm feeling so strange," Echo spluttered.

"It's just your merbody adjusting to the different pressure in the water," Kiki said, remembering Dr. Mousteau's talk. She tried not to think about the whales up above. *I could still turn around and swim back to school,* she thought, but at that moment Shelly gripped Kiki's hand even more tightly.

"Close your eyes when you get to the top, so the sun won't blind you," Shelly said, reminding her friends of Mrs. Karp's surface instructions. "Open them carefully when you feel the sun's heat." The girls quickly closed their eyes.

Suddenly a loud shriek filled the water: *MOOOOOOOWHAWK!* The sound vibrated throughout Kiki's body.

"What's that noise?" Echo squeaked.

Kiki and Echo froze, but Shelly pulled them along. "It's the male humpback's song," she explained.

"Whales sing?" Echo asked, still squeezing her eyes shut. "I don't remember that from my second-grade report."

"Of course they sing," Shelly said excitedly. "Didn't you hear Dr. Mousteau's lecture? Grandpa told me they have the longest songs of any creature."

"I wonder if the humans are near and can hear it too," Echo said. "Swim faster so we can see for ourselves!"

Splash! The class broke through the surface of the ocean.

Kiki felt the burst of air on her face. She felt the pleasant warmth of the sun.

"Students, slowly open your eyes," Mrs. Karp instructed. Kiki did as she was told. Little by little, she opened her eyes.

And then she screamed and screamed!

No More Secrets

AAAAAH!" KIKI HOWLED OUT.
"AAAAAH!"

"What's wrong?" Echo asked.

"What is that?" Kiki cried, and pointed to an oval object, shiny and huge.

"It's just an eye," Shelly laughed.

Kiki stopped screaming. "That's the biggest eyeball I've ever seen. Let's get out of here!" she said, and started to dive.

"Wait!" Shelly said. "Where are you going? What's wrong? I thought you liked whales."

Kiki started to cry. "Are you kidding? I'm petrified of them! I can't believe how big they are!"

Shelly and Echo looked at each other in surprise. "Why didn't you tell us?" Echo asked.

"Are you merladies all right?" Mrs. Karp asked, looking sharply at Kiki.

"Of course," Shelly quickly answered. "Kiki was just startled by how big this whale is."

Big didn't begin to describe the creature in front of Kiki. It was massive! Part of it floated above the water, and that part was as big as ten ordinary merhouses put together. The whale had large creases in its neck, and Kiki saw two huge scars on its side. For a moment, she felt sorry that the whale had been hurt. But then she went back to being scared again.

All around her, she could hear excited merkids shouting. "Wow, this one is like an island!" Rocky yelled.

"Ick!" Pearl screeched. "This one is covered with barnacles."

"Mine is the biggest one ever!" Adam shouted.

Kiki's eyes darted around. There must

have been at least twenty enormous humpbacks in this pod. Just then, one of them spouted water from its blowhole and showered the kids.

"I think that whale just spit on us!" Rocky yelled.

Kiki wanted to race home as fast as possible. But she was frozen in place. "Please don't tell anyone in class how scared I am," she whispered to Shelly and Echo. "Especially Pearl and Rocky. Pearl will make fun of me, and Rocky will tease me about how scared and small I am."

"Kiki," Shelly said, "don't worry. Relax. The whales won't hurt you. I promise. "

"And we won't tell anyone your secret.

It's safe with us. I bet you a lot of merkids are frightened—more than you think," Echo said reassuringly. "I still am, a little bit."

Then Kiki heard Shelly speaking to the whale. And even though Kiki was terrified to the tip of her tail, she understood every word.

"Hello," Shelly said. "We are excited to meet you. May we touch you?"

"It winked at us!" Echo said with a nervous giggle.

"It's soooooo huge," Kiki said quietly. It was true. The girls weren't even as big as this whale's flippers. "One smack of its tail and we'd go flying."

"Don't worry. He's very gentle," Shelly
said. She reached out her hand toward the
enormous whale.

"Don't touch him!" Kiki yelled. But Shelly patted the whale and spoke to him again. The whale let out a sound like a moan.

"Really?" Shelly answered.

"What did he say?" Echo said. "Did Dr. Mousteau teach us those words?"

"He said, 'It's okay,'" Kiki explained.

"What's okay?" Echo asked.

"This," Shelly said. "Watch!"

8

Whale Ride

S HELLY!" KIKI SCREAMED. "GET down off that whale! You'll get hurt!"

Shelly waved from the whale's back, her long red hair swirling around her. "He said we could all ride him."

"Wow! Come on, Kiki, let's do it. Maybe we'll see a boat or something human!" Echo said.

"We'll fall off!" Kiki answered.

"No, we won't," Shelly said. "Kiki, Echo, meet Mortimer. He said we can hold on to his bumps." Shelly pointed to three knobs on the back of the humpback's head.

"Well, you can just tell Mortimer that you are not going to do any such thing," Kiki said desperately. "Mrs. Karp will not allow it."

Kiki, Shelly, and Echo quickly looked at Mrs. Karp, who was trying to keep Rocky from pulling another whale's tail.

"She didn't say we couldn't ride a whale," Shelly said.

Echo grinned as Mortimer let out another long moan.

Kiki folded her arms over her chest. "Mrs. Karp never told us not to ride a shark, either, but we're smart enough not to try that."

"This is different," Shelly said. "Mortimer invited us."

"I'm doing it," Echo said, surprising both Shelly and Kiki. "I may never get another chance to do anything like this again."

"No!" Kiki squealed. "Echo, you're going to get up on that monster?"

"He's not a monster," Echo said. "Just because he's big doesn't mean he's a monster."

Kiki knew Echo was right. She didn't like feeling this way. Maybe it was because she was so small herself. Or maybe it was the scary stories her brothers had told her about whales. For whatever reason, she couldn't help being afraid.

"Come on," Shelly begged. "He's really nice. He wants you to come too."

"Well, maybe," Kiki muttered. Maybe if she held on to her lucky starfish, she could safely join Shelly and Echo. She went to open her purse to get her charm . . . but the purse wasn't there! Her purse and her lucky starfish were gone!

Kiki jumped away from the whale. *Oh no!* "I . . . I can't!" She really couldn't go, not without her good-luck charm.

"Then stand back," Shelly said, "because here we go!"

Echo jumped onto Mortimer, behind Shelly. "I can't believe I'm doing this," Echo said with a nervous giggle.

With a flip of his tail, Mortimer sprayed Kiki with a big splash of water. Then Mortimer, Echo, and Shelly were gone.

9

Deep-Sea Danger

WHEEE!" SHELLY, ECHO, AND Mortimer dove deep into the ocean.

"Come back!" Kiki yelled, but her voice was lost in whale song. All around her, whales sang. Kiki held her hands over her ears to block out the noise. "We've got to stop them. They're going to be hurt! Won't someone help me?" Kiki cried.

Everyone was too busy talking, touching, splashing, and learning about the other whales. No one heard Kiki. She couldn't see Mrs. Karp anywhere.

"I have to find her," Kiki said. She rushed between the huge whales, searching desperately for her teacher. "Where did she go?"

With no sign of Mrs. Karp, Kiki was frantic. She realized she would have to be the one to save her friends—there wasn't a second to waste. Up went her tail, and down went her head into the water.

Whoosh!

Mortimer raced by. Kiki swam as fast

as she could, but a small mergirl is no match for a speeding humpback whale.

As she got closer, she heard her friends screaming.

"Oh no!" Kiki said. "They're in danger! I knew it!

"Help!" she yelled. "Somebody help me!" *If only I hadn't lost my starfish,* she thought, *none of this would have happened!*

"I can help," a voice said.

Kiki came face to face with . . . a whale!

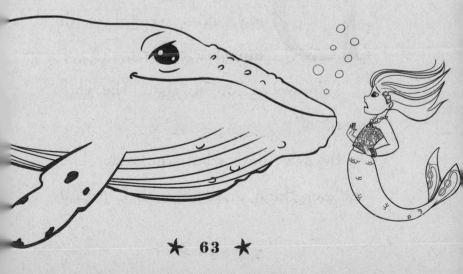

A Big Decision

DON'T EAT ME! DON'T HURT me!" Kiki pleaded in the humpback dialect.

"Why would you say that?" the whale asked.

"Because that's what whales do. They eat everything in their sight. Especially small things. Like me," Kiki whimpered, and backed away. This whale was only half as big as Mortimer, but that was still too large for Kiki.

"Please don't leave," the little whale said. "I've never met a mergirl before. And all these merkids are splashing and making so much noise, they're scaring me!"

Kiki stopped. "What? You're scared? How could something as tremendous as you be scared of something as little as me?"

"I'm just a baby whale," he said. "But my uncle Mortimer always told me to help all creatures of the sea. And you were calling for help. What's wrong?"

Kiki couldn't believe her ears. "*Wow!*" she said. "You sure are big for a baby."

Surprising herself, she didn't swim away. After all, the baby whale was kind of cute. Kiki continued, "Your uncle sped away with my friends on his back. They're in danger, and I've got to find them now!"

"If you want, you can hold on to my tail and we'll go look for them," said the young whale. "But you should know that my uncle would never harm anyone. You can ask any of the whales in our pod."

Kiki wasn't sure what to do. She didn't want to touch or go near this whale, but she had to save Shelly and Echo. Slowly she put her fingers around his left fluke. He didn't feel icky at all. Kiki was surprised to find that his fin was pretty smooth.

"My name is Orman. Hold tightly—I
won't swim too fast," he assured her.

"I-I'm K-Kiki," she stammered as
Orman dove deep into the water. At first,
Kiki was so nervous she squeezed her eyes

shut. She felt the water rushing past her cheeks. After a few minutes, she dared to open one eye.

The undersea world swirled by in a colorful blur. It wasn't scary at all. It was really very pretty. Kiki was having so much fun, she almost forgot she was searching for her friends. Suddenly a mass of bubbles swirled around her and Orman.

"Kiki!" Shelly and Echo yelled.

"Shelly! Echo!" Kiki shouted back. "Where have you been?" She shook a finger at them. "You could have been injured! You could have lost a fin! You are both so lucky Orman and I were able to find you."

Mortimer let out a hearty laughing sound. Shelly and Echo joined in.

"What are you all laughing at?" Kiki asked. "This is serious!"

"Save us from what?" Echo asked.

"From . . . from that huge whale," Kiki said. "He—he might eat you."

Shelly smiled. "Oh, Kiki, thank you for being so brave and trying to help us. But we don't need saving."

"You don't?" Kiki said.

"No," Shelly said. "We were having fun."

"Then why were you screaming when Mortimer took off with you?" Kiki asked.

"Screaming? We were squealing because we were so excited," Echo told her. "But I'm sorry we left you alone. I forgot that you weren't feeling well."

"And that you were scared," Shelly said. "But, Kiki, if you're so terrified of humpbacks, why are you with one now?"

Kiki looked from Orman to her friends and explained, "His name is Orman, and he's only a young whale. I would never ride on his back. I only held on to his fluke, and he wasn't swimming all that fast. . . ."

Shelly laughed. Then Echo. And then Mortimer and Orman. Kiki was mad for a second, but then she laughed too.

"Well, at least we don't have to ride the whales anymore," she said. "I'm not as frightened as I was at first, and Orman is really nice, but now we can all go home."

Shelly and Echo smiled and shook their heads.

"There's one more adventure today," Echo said. "Mortimer is going to breach with us on his back."

"No!" Kiki said.

"Yes!" Shelly said. "And you can do it too."

"I would never," Kiki said.

"If you don't do it, you'll never know the fun you're missing," Echo said. "This may be your only chance to do something this exciting."

Shelly held out her hand. "Come on, Kiki."

Kiki looked at Shelly's hand and made

her decision. "I can't. I'm terrified of such a large creature," she said in the humpback dialect. "I'm sorry, Mortimer; I'm sorry, Orman, but I just can't help myself. Maybe it's because I've always been so little for my age." Kiki began to cry. "And . . . I lost my lucky starfish charm."

"We'll help you look for it," Shelly said immediately.

"No," Kiki said, wiping her tears. "You go have fun. You may never get this chance again."

"I'll help you," Orman told Kiki.

Kiki couldn't help smiling at the cute whale. Once again, she held on to his tail. He swam toward the bottom of the ocean. Every couple of yards, he would stop so

Kiki could look behind the red-and-yellow coral reefs, on the spiny purple sea urchins, and around the sea cucumbers.

"Orman, do you think we'll ever find it?" Kiki asked him. "It's special because my mermom gave it to me."

And just then, on top of a barrel sponge, Kiki spotted her shell purse!

"Stop, Orman! I see it!" Kiki said. She swam to the barrel sponge, picked up her purse, and took out the starfish.

"This is my lucky charm, Orman," she said, showing him the five-pointed star. She knew she would never have found it without his help. "And you're my lucky friend. Now let's go for that ride!"

11

Flying

CAREFULLY, KIKI GOT ON Orman's back and grabbed a knob on his head.

"Don't worry, Kiki," Orman said. "I won't go too fast."

Up they swam, back to Shelly, Echo,

and Mortimer. Kiki's friends couldn't believe their eyes!

"Kiki, you look awesome!" Shelly cheered. "Are you ready? Hold on tight."

"Ready!" Kiki answered. "Thanks for waiting for me." She was still a little nervous, but she knew Orman and her friends would look out for her.

Mortimer spoke to Orman, and Orman slapped his tail. Suddenly water zoomed past the girls' faces and they were propelled toward the surface much faster than any merperson could ever swim.

"*Aaaaah!*" screamed Kiki, her eyes shut tight.

"Mrs. Karp!" Rocky yelled. "Look at Kiki, Shelly, and Echo!"

A huge gasp came from the rest of their class. "Girls!" Mrs. Karp called.

Kiki heard Rocky and Mrs. Karp, but she couldn't let go. She held on as Orman cleared the water and they soared into the air.

"Wow!" Shelly said from Mortimer's back. "This is amazing. Kiki, open your eyes. You don't want to miss this."

Kiki opened one eye as the wind blew her long dark hair. Mortimer and Orman had breached together. "It's beautiful," Kiki breathed.

As far as she could see, blue water stretched all around. Up above, bright

sky matched the sparkling sea.

"We're swimming in the air!" Echo screamed. And they were. For just a minute. And then they started falling.

"Don't let go!" Shelly yelled.

Kiki squeezed Orman's knob hard. The water felt like a rock when they hit it, and it was all Kiki could do to stay on Orman's back. But she did. And right beside her, she could see that Shelly and Echo had stayed on Mortimer.

When they were safely back under the water, Echo giggled. "We did it!"

Kiki couldn't believe it. Thanks to Orman and her merfriends, she had done something she'd never thought she could do. She hugged Orman. "Thank you, my lucky pal. I hope I get to see you again."

Orman winked at Kiki, and Kiki knew she had a friend for life.

12

Trouble Time?

YOU ARE IN SO MUCH TROUBLE!" Rocky told the girls after their whale rides.

"Yeah," added Pearl. "No more ocean trips for you. Ha!"

Mrs. Karp blew the conch shell, signaling that it was time to leave. All the merstudents gathered around her. Kiki gulped when Mrs. Karp glared at her.

"All right, class," Mrs. Karp said. "Let's descend."

Nobody said a word as they swam downward together. It took a minute for their eyes to adjust to the darkness, and Echo jumped when a small basketweave cusk-eel slithered by her.

"Let's assemble in the classroom," Mrs. Karp told the class. "We have a few more minutes left before the end of the school day."

The merstudents groaned. "I thought she would let us go home early," Shelly whispered.

"Nope," Rocky said, swimming by the three mergirls. "She wants to yell at you first."

Kiki glanced at Mrs. Karp, who had a serious look on her face. Kiki was afraid Rocky was right.

"What do you think Mrs. Karp will do

to us?" Echo whispered as the class floated

down the hallway.

Kiki shrugged. Her parents wouldn't

mind that she'd ridden Orman, but they

would be upset if she got in trouble at school. They always told her to do her best in her studies, but that even if she couldn't get good grades, she could behave herself. It had been a huge honor for her to win a Trident Academy scholarship. She was the first one in her family to attend the prestigious school. It would be terrible if she was sent home in disgrace. Kiki held her breath as Mrs. Karp addressed the class.

"You may take a few minutes to write about the humpback whales," she said. All the merkids bent over their pieces of seaweed to begin their essays. Everyone except Rocky.

"What about Kiki, Shelly, and Echo?"

Rocky asked. "Aren't they going to get sent to the headmaster for riding those whales?"

Mrs. Karp stared at Rocky and then at the girls. Kiki felt sick to her stomach again. "There is one regrettable part about today's ocean trip," Mrs. Karp said.

Kiki waited anxiously as Mrs. Karp paused.

"I am terribly disappointed that I did not get to ride the whales," Mrs. Karp told them. "I have always wanted to breach with a humpback."

Kiki looked at her teacher in surprise. "You mean we aren't in trouble?" she asked.

Mrs. Karp shook her head. "Not this

time." Then she smiled and continued, "But if the humpbacks ever come back, I expect a ride."

"Of course," Kiki quickly told her teacher. "Orman, my new whale friend,

would be delighted." Kiki's lucky starfish charm sat on top of her desk. With the charm, and with the help of Shelly, Echo, and Orman, she had faced her biggest fear. Kiki smiled and wrote her essay. She couldn't wait for her next big adventure at Trident Academy.

Class Reports

★ ✦ ★

MY ESSAY ON HUMPBACK WHALES

By Shelly Siren

Today I did something I have only dreamed about. I got to breach on top of a humpback whale. It was amazing. The whale, whose name is Mortimer, was so big he made me feel like a tiny speck of the littlest krill.

MY ESSAY ON HUMPBACK WHALES

By Echo Reef

I learned that humpback whales sing very loud songs. I think their songs are kind of sad, like they are missing a loved one. Humpback whales have the longest songs of any sea creature. They are also very friendly to mermaids. I was sorry we didn't get to see a human, but I will never forget riding a whale.

MY ESSAY ON HUMPBACK WHALES

By Rocky Ridge

At first, I thought the humpback whales were really ugly. After all, they have bumps all over their faces. But when I saw one jump out of the water, I thought it was really pretty.

MY ESSAY ON HUMPBACK WHALES
By Pearl Swamp

Humpback whales are the biggest, grossest, most disgusting creatures in the ocean. They are noisy and stinky. I hope I never have to see another one ever again. I don't think it's fair that some people in our class didn't get in trouble for doing something they shouldn't have done. And it wasn't right that they didn't share with us. If one person got to ride on a whale, then everyone should get to ride on a whale. It's only fair.

MY ESSAY ON HUMPBACK WHALES
By Kiki Coral

I was terrified of being around the biggest creatures in the ocean. I thought because they were big, they would be mean. But they were very nice and understanding.

I enjoyed looking around when we breached. I could see the blue of the ocean going on forever. All around us, the sky matched the blue. I felt like a seabird soaring high above the world.

Mrs. Karp, I hope Mortimer and his nephew, Orman, come back for a visit. It would be fun to ride on a whale with you! I would still be a little scared, but not terrified.

The Mermaid Tales Song

REFRAIN:

Let the water roar

Deep down we're swimming along

Twirling, swirling, singing the mermaid song.

VERSE 1:

Shelly flips her tail

Racing, diving, chasing a whale

Twirling, swirling, singing the mermaid song.

VERSE 2:

Pearl likes to shine

Oh my Neptune, she looks so fine

Twirling, swirling, singing the mermaid song.

VERSE 3:

Shining Echo flips her tail

Backward and forward without fail

Twirling, swirling, singing the mermaid song.

VERSE 4:

Amazing Kiki

Far from home and floating so free

Twirling, swirling, singing the mermaid song.

Author's Note

OCEANS ARE FANTASTIC PLACES filled with incredible creatures, like humpback whales. Check out the fangtooth or the hairy angler if you want to see something really creepy! Maybe there are other living things we haven't found yet that are even more amazing—like mermaids! Read on for some facts about the ocean animals mentioned in this book. Hope I didn't miss any! Tell me about your favorite sea creature by writing me on the Kids Talk to Debbie section of www.debbiedadey.com. Is your favorite a baby whale, like Orman?

My nephew Damon Gibson actually swam with humpbacks and told me it was one of the coolest experiences of his life. If you don't know how to swim, I hope you'll learn. After all, you may get to swim with whales one day!

Take care,
Debbie Dadey

Glossary

BARREL SPONGE: This huge sponge is large enough for a person to hide inside!

BASKETWEAVE CUSK-EEL: This eel has been found at depths of 26,000 feet, the greatest depth for any fish.

BOTTLENOSE DOLPHIN: These dolphins vary in color from pale blue to slate gray. They "talk" using whistles, clicks, and squeaks.

CONCH: The conch shell has been collected because of its beauty, and the conch itself has been eaten for food. Conchs are now at risk for extinction.

FANGTOOTH: This deep-water fish has a large head and massive teeth.

GRAY HERON: This gray-backed bird will wait patiently for a long time and then stab quickly with its bill to catch a fish.

GREAT WHITE SHARK: Great whites have been known to attack humans, but we are not their natural prey. Scientists believe that the attacking shark mistakes the human for a seal or a turtle. It is important to stay out of the ocean during early-morning and early-evening hours, when sharks are more likely to feed.

HAIRY ANGLER: Only a few of these weird-looking fish have ever been seen. The hairy angler has a huge mouth, little eyes, and long, thin fin rays, making it look like a bald man with a few wild hairs.

HUMPBACK WHALE: Humpback whales grow to be between forty and fifty feet long. How big is that? Many kids' bedrooms are around ten feet long. That would mean one whale could be five times as long as your bedroom!

JEWEL ANEMONE: These colorful creatures make a fabulously colorful display on underwater cliffs and can be any color, although pink and yellow are common.

KILLER WHALE: Killer whales are not whales at all. They are the largest member of the dolphin family. Despite their name, killer whales are not known for attacking people—or mermaids—in the wild.

KRILL: Antarctic krill are very important in the southern ocean food chain.

OCTOPUS: The small blue-ringed octopus makes enough toxic spit to kill a human! It has little bright blue circles all over its body.

PINK CORAL: Corals are some of the brightest reef creatures. They can be pink, red, orange, yellow, or white.

POLKA-DOT BATFISH: The batfish is an oddly shaped fish that uses its fins to walk over the ocean floor.

PURPLE SEA URCHIN: This small urchin loves to eat kelp. In fact, urchins have destroyed parts of giant kelp forests.

SEA CUCUMBER: This wormlike creature eats mud and sand!

SHRIMP: There are many types of shrimp in the ocean. The peacock mantis shrimp is brightly colored and lives in warm water near reefs.

STARFISH: The vivid colors of starfish scare off some predators.

TUBE SPONGE: This pinkish sponge looks like fingers reaching up from the sea floor.

FIND OUT WHAT HAPPENS IN THE NEXT . . .

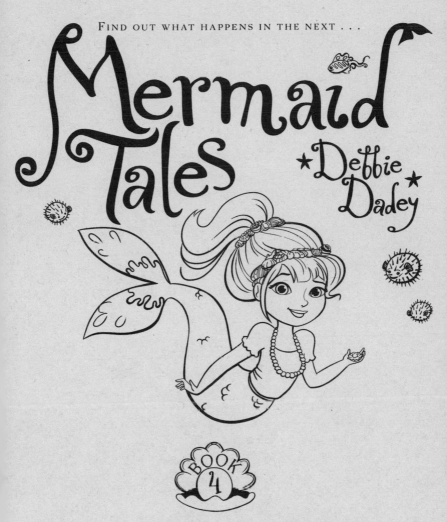

Mermaid Tales ★ Debbie Dadey ★

BOOK 4

Danger in the Deep Blue Sea

Late-Breaking News!

"OH MY NEPTUNE!" PEARL Swamp shrieked as she swam into the huge front hallway of Trident Academy. "Did you see the newspaper this morning?"

Wanda Slug, Pearl's good friend, shook

her head. "No, I didn't," she said. "I had to finish my homework before school." The two mergirls floated out of the way of some fourth-grade merboys who zoomed past them.

Trident Academy was a prestigious school in Trident City. Third-grade through tenth-grade merkids came from all over the ocean to study in the enormous clamshell. The front hall alone was big enough for a humpback whale to take a nap in.

Pearl's blond hair and long strand of pearls swirled in the water as everyone rushed around her to get to their classrooms. "My dad made me read the front page," she told Wanda. "You'll never believe it! There have been shark sightings in Trident City!"

"What?" Wanda gasped. "Are you kidding? That's terrible." Sharks were the number one danger to the merpeople community.

Pearl's green eyes widened. "I'm serious. I couldn't even swim here by myself. My father hired a Shark Patrol guard to escort me to and from school."

Wanda shuddered. "I'm glad I live in the Trident Academy dorm. I wouldn't want to be swimming home with a shark on my tail." Both girls looked at their mertails and wiggled them gently. Neither girl noticed that the front hall was almost empty of merstudents.

Pearl slapped her gold tail on the shell floor and folded her arms across her chest. "This is ridiculous. What's wrong with this place? Can't they keep scary sharks from chasing people? Something should be done."

"Yeah, but what can we do?" Wanda said. "We're just third graders."

Pearl twisted her necklace in her fingers. "I hate being scared, and I hate having a Shark Guard. My dad might not even let me go to Tail Flippers practice if things get worse!"

"No!" Wanda gasped. Tail Flippers was the school's dance and gymnastics team.

Pearl sighed. "I don't know what I'm going to do, but I'm going to do something. I refuse to let sharks ruin my life."

"Uh-oh," Wanda said, finally noticing the empty hall. "We'd better get to class, or *Mrs. Karp* will ruin our lives!"

Debbie Dadey

is the author and coauthor of one hundred and fifty children's books, including the series The Adventures of the Bailey School Kids. A former teacher and librarian, Debbie now lives in Bucks County, Pennsylvania, with her wonderful husband and children. They live about two hours from the ocean and love to go there to look for mermaids. If you see any, let her know at www.debbiedadey.com.

Break out your sleeping bag and best pajamas. . . . You're invited!

Sleepover Squad

❀ Collect them all! ❀

Candy Fairies

Visit candyfairies.com for more delicious fun with your favorite fairies.

Play games, download activities, and so much more!

Nancy Drew and The Clue Crew

Test your detective skills with more Clue Crew cases!

#1 *Sleepover Sleuths*

#2 *Scream for Ice Cream*

#3 *Pony Problems*

#4 *The Cinderella Ballet Mystery*

#5 *Case of the Sneaky Snowman*

#6 *The Fashion Disaster*

#7 *The Circus Scare*

#8 *Lights, Camera . . . Cats!*

#9 *The Halloween Hoax*

#10 *Ticket Trouble*

#11 *Ski School Sneak*

#12 *Valentine's Day Secret*

#13 *Chick-napped!*

#14 *The Zoo Crew*

#15 *Mall Madness*

#16 *Thanksgiving Thief*

#17 *Wedding Day Disaster*

#18 *Earth Day Escapade*

#19 *April Fool's Day*

#20 *Treasure Trouble*

#21 *Double Take*

#22 *Unicorn Uproar*

#23 *Babysitting Bandit*

#24 *Princess Mix-up Mystery*

#25 *Buggy Breakout*

#26 *Camp Creepy*

#27 *Cat Burglar Caper*

#28 *Time Thief*

#29 *Designed for Disaster*

#30 *Dance Off*

#31 *The Make-a-Pet Mystery*

#32 *Cape Mermaid Mystery*

#33 *The Pumpkin Patch Puzzle*

FROM ALADDIN • PUBLISHED BY SIMON & SCHUSTER